ORDINARY GEORGE

Reading Ladder

For Zac,

who is extraordinary and excellent

J.N.

For Marina and Fernan

L.S.

EGMONT

We bring stories to life

Book Band: Turquoise

First published in Great Britain 2016
by Egmont UK Ltd
The Yellow Building, 1 Nicholas Road, London W11 4AN
Text copyright © Joanna Nadin 2016
Illustrations copyright © Lucía Serrano 2016
The author and illustrator have asserted their moral rights.
ISBN 978 1 4052 75422
www.egmont.co.uk
A CIP catalogue record for this title is available from the British Library.
Printed in Singapore.
58742/1

Stay safe online. Any website addresses listed in this book are correct at the time of going to print.
However, Egmont is not responsible for content hosted by third parties. Please be aware that
online content can be subject to change and websites can contain content that is unsuitable for
children. We advise that all children are supervised when using the internet.

ORDINARY GEORGE

JOANNA NADIN

ILLustrated by

LUCÍA SERRANO

Everything about the Jones family was extraordinary.

Mr Jones was an incredible inventor, who had created the world's first time machine out of a bus, some tin foil and an alarm clock.

Mrs Jones was an exceptional explorer, who had discovered the long lost tomb of King Parabola.

Daisy Jones was a terrific trumpeter, who had mastered seventy-two symphonies by the time she was four.

Grandpa Jones held the record for the world's longest nose hair (at four and a half centimetres).

Even Digger the dog was no ordinary animal. He could jump through hoops of fire, and dance a can-can in a tutu and a fancy hat.

Yes, everything about the Jones family was extraordinary. Everything, that is, except George.

George Jones hadn't discovered anything.

His nose hair was normal length.

He couldn't play the trumpet . . .

or jump through hoops . . .

. . . or dance the can-can.

The only thing he had invented was
cheese and chocolate on toast,
and not even Digger would eat that.

No, George was completely and utterly
ordinary. And he hated it.

'I wish I had earlobes that reached down to my toes,' he said to his dad.

'Oh, you are funny, George,' laughed Dad.

'I wish I could fly to the moon in my pyjamas,' he said to his mum.

'Oh you are funny, George,' laughed Mum.

'I wish I could eat a pizza as big as this house without being sick,' he said to his sister Daisy.

'Oh, you are funny, George,' laughed
Daisy.

But George never saw the funny side.

17

One day George was trying to see if he was the world's greatest kazoo player.

He wasn't.

'Don't worry, George,' said Grandpa. 'Everyone is really good at something. There's plenty of time left to find out what makes you extraordinary.'

But there wasn't plenty of time at all.

The class talent show was in just five days and everyone was taking part.

Lacey Ledbetter was going to play the national anthem on milk bottles.

Bruce Biggs was going to juggle three
oranges and a toy monkey.

And Cordelia Crisp was going to
swallow a goldfish whole and burp it
back up again.

'You'll be right as rain, George,' said Grandpa. 'You just need to try a new thing every day.'

And so he did.

On Monday, George tried to beat the world record for squishing marshmallows into his mouth. But there were only a few left in the packet, so he stuck them to his face instead.

'You are funny, George,' laughed Mum.

But George didn't see the funny side.
'There's always tomorrow,' said
Grandpa.
'I suppose,' sighed George. And went
to bed.

On Tuesday, George tried to learn the names of all the planets in the solar system, in song. But he could only remember Mars and Jupiter, so he had to make up the others.

'I don't think Magicpants and Kerpiffle are planets,' laughed Dad. 'Though you are funny, George.'

But George didn't see the funny side.

'There's always tomorrow,' said Grandpa.

'I suppose,' sighed George.

And went to bed.

On Wednesday, George tried to do a head stand whilst balancing pineapples on his feet. One pineapple rolled under the sofa. The other rolled into Digger the dog. And then so did George.

28

'You are funny, George,' laughed
Daisy.

But George didn't see the funny side
(and nor did Digger).

'There's always tomorrow,' said
Grandpa.

'I suppose,' sighed George.

And went to bed.

On Thursday, George learned balloon
modelling and tried to make a giraffe,
an alligator and a chimpanzee.
But they all looked the same.
'You are funny, George,'
laughed everyone.

But George didn't see the funny side.

'There's always tomorrow,' said Grandpa.

'I suppose,' sighed George.

And went to bed.

Grandpa was wrong. There was no tomorrow.

Because when George woke up, tomorrow was today and today was Friday and Friday was the day of the talent show.

'What am I going to do?' George moaned. 'Marshmallows don't stick to faces very well, I made up most of the planets in the solar system song, my pineapple head stand is a danger zone and my balloon animals all look like worms. I'll be the laughing stock of the school.'

'That's it!' cried Grandpa.

'What's it?' sighed George.

'George, I have a plan, and it's a right bobby dazzler.'

'That is the worst plan ever,' said George when Grandpa had told him his plan. 'I'll be laughed right out of town.'

'Don't be so sure,' said Mum.

'It could just work,' agreed Daisy.

'And if it doesn't, we can use the time machine to go back to yesterday and you can try yodeling instead,' said Dad.

George didn't see the funny side. But it was the only plan he had, and so he decided he had better use it.

The talent show was the talk of the school. The whole class was on the edge of their seats with excitement and even Mrs Buttlewhip, the headmistress, had come to watch.

Lacey Ledbetter played the national anthem on milk bottles and everyone whooped.

Bruce Biggs juggled three oranges and a
toy monkey and everyone cheered.

But Cordelia Crisp wasn't allowed to swallow a goldfish. Mrs Buttlewhip said eating pets was against all sorts of rules. So instead she burped her way through the alphabet and everyone clapped.

GAAAARB

Finally, it was George's turn.

George took his place at the centre of the stage. Then he began.

'And now I, Extraordinary George, will perform a feat of daring before your very eyes. I will be the first ever boy to sing a song about the solar system standing on my head with marshmallows on my face whilst balancing pineapples on my feet and modelling animals from balloons.'

And he did.

And he did something else too.

Lacey Ledbetter was the first to get the giggles.

Then Bruce Biggs began to guffaw.

Next Cordelia Crisp doubled up in laughter.

44

Until everyone in the room was
laughing so much they were crying.
Even Mrs Buttlewhip, who had to be
given a glass of water and a biscuit to
calm her down.

'You really are funny, George,' she said,
when she had finally stopped chuckling.

'Yes, you really, really are,' agreed
Bruce Biggs.

'The funniest person ever,' smiled
Lacey Ledbetter.

'In the whole world,' agreed Cordelia
Crisp, who never normally agreed
about anything.

'Extraordinary,' Mrs Buttlewhip
said as she handed George the prize.

'That's the only word for it. You are
extraordinary, George.'

And for once George saw
the funny side.